LITTLE MONSTERS

LITTLE MONSTERS

M. JEAN CRAIG

The Dial Press · New York

Library of Congress Cataloging in Publication Data
Craig, M Jean. Little monsters.
Summary: Descriptions of eighteen animals, all small enough to hold in
your hand, with blown-up photographs that make them look monstrous.
1. Animals—Miscellanea—Juvenile literature.
[1. Animals—Miscellanea] I. Title.
QL49.C7 1977 591 76-42936
ISBN 0-8037-4727-6   ISBN 0-8037-4728-4 lib. bdg.

Photographs appear courtesy of:
Jacket photo and p. 31: James H. Robinson / Photo Researchers;
title page and 7: Lynwood M. Chace / National Audubon Society /
Photo Researchers; 9: Bruce J. Hayward; 11: C. Roessler / Sea Library;
13: Ross E. Hutchins; 15: M. W. Larson; 17: Lilo Hess;
19: (top) Carl W. Rettenmeyer, (bottom) Edward S. Ross;
21: Diane R. Nelson and Robert Schuster; 23: Stanley and Kay Breeden;
25: William A. Amos; 27: S. Beaufoy;
29: Trinidad Regional Virus Laboratory, courtesy Arthur M. Greenhall;
33: Loomis Dean / Time-Life Picture Agency © Time, Inc.;
35: Peter David / Photo Researchers; 37: Russ Kinne / Photo Researchers;
39: A. van den Nieuwenhuizen Dierenfotograaf.

The pictures of these little "monsters" are just as large as we could make them so you could see how frightening they look. Not one of these animals is really more than six inches long, and most of them are much, much smaller.

SPICEBUSH SWALLOWTAIL BUTTERFLY LARVA

This is not a snake with enormous eyes, nor is it the head of a sea-serpent. It is only a caterpillar, or larva, as long as the word "c a t e r p i l l a r" on this page, and soon it will become a butterfly.

Those huge "eyes" are not eyes at all, but colored spots on the caterpillar's skin. The real eyes are very small, and are hidden underneath the head. Perhaps the colored spots frighten away the birds or lizards that are the caterpillar's natural enemies.

The spicebush swallowtail butterfly larva is found in the eastern part of the United States and Canada.

6

VAMPIRE BAT

Almost everyone has heard of vampire bats, but most people think they are huge bats that suck all the blood from animals and people and kill them.

This is a real vampire bat, and its furry body is only about three inches long. The vampire does live on blood, but it does not need very much blood. It uses its flat front teeth to scrape a thin layer of skin from a sleeping animal, such as a cow, until a few drops of blood ooze out. The vampire rolls its tiny tongue into the shape of a tube and scoops up the blood. Then it flies quietly away. The animal usually doesn't even wake up.

Vampire bats are not altogether harmless, though, since they can spread diseases from one animal to another.

PORCUPINE FISH

The prickly porcupine fish isn't always all puffed up. This one has swallowed air or water, making itself about twice its normal size, and looking very dangerous. This may stop other larger fish from trying to eat it.

But porcupine fish, even after they blow themselves up, are only as big as a softball, and they are not dangerous at all. In fact, they are so gentle and tame that many people keep them in aquariums.

At feeding time, a porcupine fish will go to the top of the water and wait for its food. Sometimes, while it is waiting, it shoots water from its beaky mouth right into the face of anyone standing near. No one is sure why—perhaps it is impatient, or perhaps this is a kind of greeting.

STAG BEETLES

A male deer with horns is called a stag, and the stag beetle's pincers look like a stag's horns.

There are thousands and thousands of different kinds of beetles in the world, and stag beetles are among the biggest. Some stag beetles that live in India are as big as a sparrow.

The stag beetles in the picture are the kind found in the United States, and they are only about two inches long. They eat bits of dead plants and animals that they find on the ground.

A male stag beetle likes to have a piece of ground all to himself. When two stag beetles meet, they fight, using their big pincers. They don't kill each other—they just knock each other about, until the loser goes away.

WOLF SPIDER

This savage wolf spider is only the size of a postage stamp—luckily!

The wolf spider doesn't make a web. It digs a hole in the ground, and then it builds a small tower of sticks and grass next to the hole. It sits on top of the tower and watches, with its eight eyes, for an insect or bug to come along. Then it pounces, and kills the insect with its poison fangs. After that it drags the insect down into the hole and sucks it dry.

The wolf spider is a fierce hunter, but a good, careful mother. It carries its babies around on its back until they are big enough to take care of themselves.

Wolf spiders can be found all over the world. There are at least 2000 kinds of them.

JACKSON'S CHAMELEON

This could be a model for a monster in a horror movie, but it is actually a live chameleon.

Most kinds of chameleons look strange, and this kind is one of the strangest. Although those long spikes seem dangerous, they can't hurt anything. The male chameleon just uses them to shove other male chameleons away when he is looking for a female.

A chameleon's tongue is longer than the chameleon is. (This chameleon is four inches long.) The tongue has a sticky tip, and the chameleon uses it for catching insects. When it sees an insect it wants to eat, it flicks its tongue out of its mouth and in again so fast that you can hardly see it move. The insect it swallows probably didn't see it at all.

A chameleon's skin changes color to match the branches or leaves it is sitting on. Then insects don't notice it waiting for them, and whatever might want to eat the chameleon has trouble finding it.

Chameleons are found in Africa, Asia, and Europe.

GIANT SPINY KATYDID
SOUTH AMERICAN KATYDID

Most katydids are less than two inches long, but these two "giants" measure over three inches from end to end. The giant spiny katydid (facing page, above) and the South American katydid (facing page, below) both live in South America, and they are related to the katydids that chirp away in the late evening during the summertime all over the United States.

Katydids rub their two front wings together to make their chirping sound. When one katydid chirps, other katydids listen. The katydid's ear is not at all where anyone might expect to find an ear. It is just a small slit on the katydid's front leg.

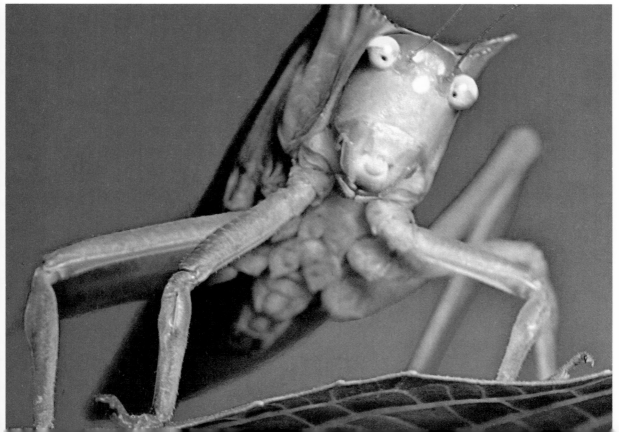

WATER BEAR

Is this a kind of giant dinosaur? No, in fact most water bears are so tiny that they can't be seen at all without a microscope. The largest water bears are only as big as a grain of sugar.

Water bears can be found all over the world. They live on the juice of plants and of other animals even smaller than they are.

The tiny water bear is very tough. Sometimes the place where it lives gets too hot, too cold, or too dry for it to stay alive. But instead of dying it dries up, shrinks into the shape of a little barrel, and waits. It doesn't die; it doesn't even get any older. It just waits.

Then when the temperature is right again, and when there is enough dampness, the water bear changes back to its original shape. Water bears can stay alive, in their dried-up barrel-shape, for over a hundred years.

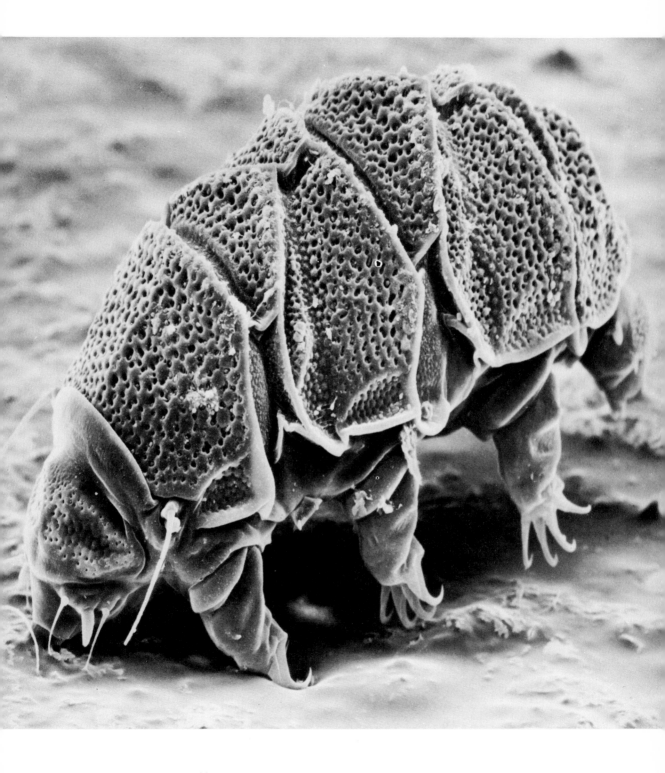

FRUIT-SUCKING MOTH LARVA

This fearsome beast is only a caterpillar that will soon become a common moth. It lives in North and South America, and its food is the juice that it sucks from ripe fruit. It is less than two inches long.

Those big circles are not eyes, but just spots of color. The larva pushes them up like that when it is touched, and then whatever is touching it is very often frightened away. The larva's real eyes are curled underneath, at the front of its head.

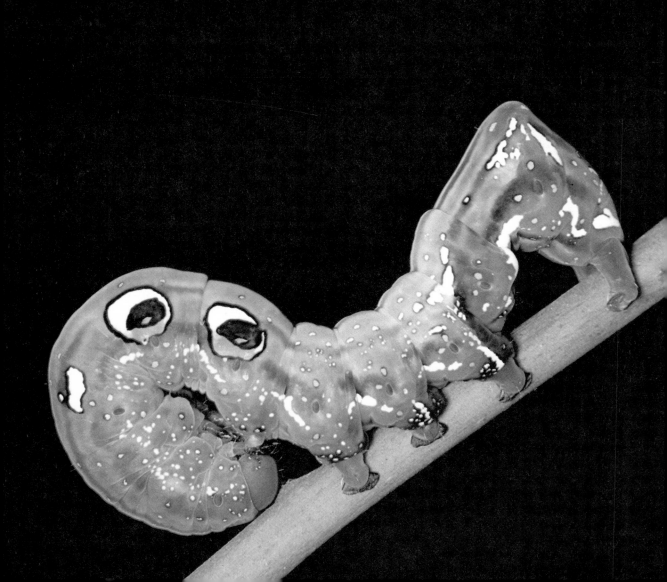

TIGER-BEETLE LARVA

There is a body behind that terrible face, but not a lot of body, for this beetle larva is not even one inch long.

But the tiger-beetle larva is just as fierce as it looks. It digs a hole in the ground and hides in it; then it pops out to grab and eat other smaller bugs that come along.

Tiger beetles live all over the world except where it is cold.

PUSS-MOTH LARVA

This caterpillar looks ready to attack a lion, but it is not even two inches long, and it never attacks anything.

To keep from being attacked or eaten itself, it sticks up those two spiky back legs that look like horns and puffs up that frightening face. Its enemies are then very likely to run away. The back legs have a bad-smelling liquid in them too, which is an extra help.

Puss-moth larvae eat leaves. This kind lives in the southern part of the United States. Later it will turn into a pretty black-and-white puss-moth.

WRINKLE-FACED BAT

In the top picture the bat looks as though it is wearing a scarf under its chin. This is really an extra fold of skin. When the bat goes to sleep, it pulls the fold of skin up over its face. Then it looks like the bottom picture.

The two dark patches on the skin-fold are thin spots, like tiny one-way windows. When the fold is pulled up, the bat can see light and dark through them, and whether anything is moving.

The wrinkle-faced bat is less than four inches long, with a head about the size of a big marble. It lives in warm climates, where it can find the fruit it likes to eat. Many are found in Mexico and Panama, but only a few have been seen in the United States.

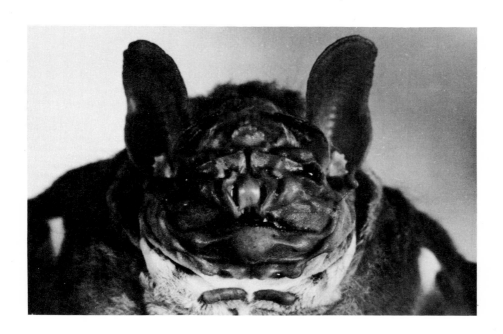

PAPER WASP

The paper wasp minds its own business, as long as it is left alone. But if it is touched, it will sting.

The paper wasp's nest is often hung from a branch, or built under the roof of a porch or even in an attic. To build its home, the paper wasp first chews up wood or plant stems to make wet paper. Then it shapes the paper into a group of little six-sided cells.

A queen wasp makes the first few cells and lays an egg in each one. Soon the eggs hatch into larvae. When the larvae become adult wasps, they add new cells to the nest, and more eggs are laid. When the eggs hatch, the adult wasps feed the larvae torn-up bits of insects. In hot weather, they bring drops of water to cool the larvae, and fan them with their wings.

Different kinds of paper wasps live all over the world. Most of them are less than an inch long.

TEXAS BANDED GECKO

This *could* be a giant dragon breathing fire. But there's no fire, of course, and a five-inch lizard is not exactly a giant—in fact, it is just big enough to curl up comfortably in a teacup.

This kind of gecko lives in Texas and some other southwestern states. It hides among the rocks in the daytime and runs about at night catching insects and spiders.

Sometimes, in hot countries, other kinds of geckos live in people's houses right along with the people. They can run up and down the walls and even across the ceilings, chasing insects, and the people are very glad to have them there because they eat up all the insects in the house.

If a Texas banded gecko is grasped by the tail, it lets the tail break off in your hand and runs away without it. It can grow a new tail again easily and quickly.

DEEP-SEA ANGLER-FISH

Angler is another word for *fisherman,* and an angler-fish is a fish that fishes for other fish.

Down in the very deepest parts of the ocean, where this angler-fish lives, it is always dark. But the female angler-fish has what looks like a light on a stick on the end of her nose, and when another fish comes along to see what is shining, the angler-fish eats it. (No one is really sure what makes that light shine.)

This deep-sea angler-fish is only three inches long, but because of its large mouth it can swallow fish twice its own size.

STAR-NOSED MOLE

It would be pretty frightening to wake up some night to find this enormous "monster" leaning over the foot of the bed. But of course the star-nosed mole is not enormous, and not monstrous at all, and it is almost never found in bedrooms!

The star-nosed mole digs tunnels in swamps or wet ground, hunting for worms or insects to eat. It uses those twenty-two tentacles around its nose to help it find food. No one knows whether it smells with the tentacles or feels with them. There is no other furry, warm-blooded animal in the world that has a nose quite like that.

The star-nosed mole can swim too, and sometimes it catches a very small fish for its dinner.

This mole is found in North America, mostly in the northeastern parts.

INFLATED FILE SHELL

An imaginary sea-monster? No, it is just an ordinary file shell, about the size of an egg, found almost anywhere in any ocean where it isn't very cold.

File shells are also called jumping shells. They jump about in the sea by squirting water through the two halves of their shell.

The long red fringes help the file shell find small sea-animals to eat.

A WORD FROM THE AUTHOR

Are these animals really "little monsters"?

They *are* little. Each one is so little that you could hold it in your hand. And they *do* have strange shapes and colors and faces, like monsters.

But a monster is not a real animal. It is something that someone has made up purposely to be frightening, like a dragon or an ogre or a three-headed Thing from Outer Space.

The animals in this book are all real animals. Each one is exactly the shape and color it has to be in order to live the way it has to live.

Nothing that is natural and real is monstrous. So of course these animals are not monsters at all.